Note to the Reader

This story includes the names of family members and friends who are very special to Pam, and this book is dedicated to them.

www.mascotbooks.com

An Alphabet Book by Mrs. Gregory's Kindergarten Class

For more information, please contact:
Mascot Books
560 Herndon Parkway #120
Herndon, VA 20170
info@mascotbooks.com

CPSIA Code: PRT0514A
ISBN-13: 9781620867129

Printed in the United States

An Alphabet Book By Mrs. Gregory's Kindergarten Class

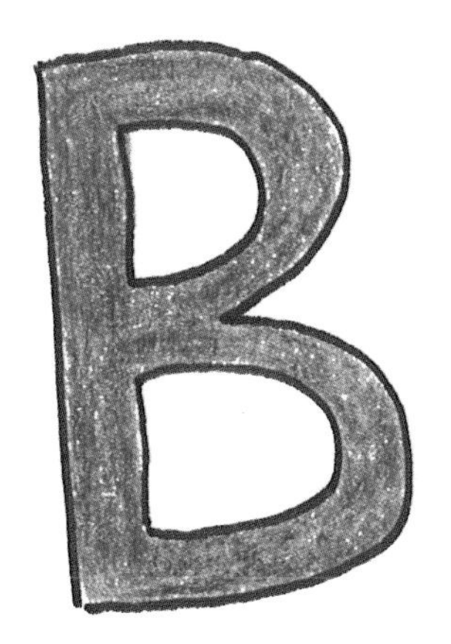

Written and Illustrated by
Pam Fisher

Molly, Jake, Ann, Allison, Jeff, Lucy, Aidan, Jeramy, Margie, and Mike are five years old, and they are in kindergarten.

They all go to Miss Julia's
Preschool and Kindergarten.

Their teacher is Mrs. Alice Gregory.

Mrs. Gregory had a special project for the children in her class. The class had to work together to think of a person's name and an object for each letter of the alphabet.

Sam
Ashley
Brendan
Angela
Jackie
Laura
Cailin
Terry
Judy
Josie
Jane
Sean
Trish
Colleen
Roy

Mrs. Gregory told the children to think
of the names of their parents, brothers,
sisters, cousins, and any other name they
could come up with, and this is their book.

Aa is for Amy and an apple.

Bb is for Beth and a baby.

Cc is for Christopher and a cat.

Dd is for David and a dog.

Ee is for Ella Kaitlin and an egg.

Ff is for Frank and a fish.

Gg is for Grandma and grapes.

Hh is for Heather and a heart.

Ii is for Isabella and ice cream.

Jj is for Jessica and a jump rope.

Kk is for Katie and a kite.

Ll is for Luke and a lollipop.

Mm is for Matthew and a moon.

Nn is for Nathan and a nest.

Oo is for Olive and an orange.

Pp is for Peyton and a pumpkin.

Qq is for Quillan and a quilt.

Rr is for Richard and a rainbow.

Ss is for Stephen and a soccer ball.

Tt is for Tyler and a tree.

Uu is for Uncle Jimmy and an umbrella.

Vv is for Vincent and a valentine.

Ww is for William and a watermelon.

Xx is for Xavier and a xylophone.

Yy is for Yolanda and a yo-yo.

Zz is for Zachary and a zebra.

Mrs. Gregory was so proud of the children. She was amazed at what a good job they all did working together.